BY DAVID ORME

illustrated by
Paul Savage

Librarian Reviewer
Joanne Bongaarts
Educational Consultant
MS in Library Media Education, Minnesota State University, Mankato, MN
Teacher and Media Specialist with Edina Public Schools, MN, 1993–2000

Reading Consultant
Elizabeth Stedem
Educator/Consultant, Colorado Springs, CO
MA in Elementary Education, University of Denver, CO

Minneapolis San Diego

First published in the United States in 2006
by Stone Arch Books,
151 Good Counsel Drive, P.O. Box 669,
Mankato, Minnesota 56002.
www.stonearchbooks.com

Originally published in Great Britain in 2004
by Badger Publishing Ltd.

Library of Congress Cataloging-in-Publication Data
Orme, David.
Something Evil / by David Orme; illustrated by Paul Savage.
p. cm.
"Keystone Books."
Summary: Despite warnings from local residents, a new city is built on the shore of a lake that has a dark secret, and when people begin to disappear, Todd and some others decide to take action.
ISBN-13: 978-1-59889-017-4 (hardcover)
ISBN-10: 1-59889-017-4 (hardcover)
[1. Monsters—Fiction. 2. Lakes—Fiction. 3. Submarines (Ships)—Fiction. 4. Horror stories.] I. Savage, Paul, 1971– ill. II. Title.
PZ7.O6338Som 2006
[Fic]—dc22 2005026563

1 2 3 4 5 6 11 10 09 08 07 06

Printed in the United States of America

Table of Contents

Chapter 1

The New City

Dark Lake was old and deep, and it was a long way from any city. People who lived in the area stayed away from the lake. They said that sometimes people who walked near Dark Lake were never seen again.

No one knew why.

Then a big, new city was planned to be built right next to the lake.

"The lake will be an important part of the city," said the builders. "People can go boating or watch the wildlife."

"It's a bad idea," local people said. "There's something evil in Dark Lake."

The city was built anyway. People from far away came to live there.

And then they started to disappear.

Chapter 2

A Murder?

The first person to disappear was a man named Jim Small. He had gone for a walk around the lake with his dog. He didn't come home. The man who lived next door called the police.

The police found Jim's dog the next day. It was at the north end of the lake, looking for its owner.

The police searched everywhere.

At last they found Jim's cap. It had bloodstains on it. The police thought he had been murdered, but there were no other clues.

At first, no one wanted to go near that part of the lake. But nothing else happened, and people forgot about it.

Then a teenager named Lisa Dahl disappeared. Some people said she had run away from home. But a friend said she saw Lisa walking near the lake on the day she disappeared.

After Lisa's disappearance, the police found a clue by the lake, close to the place where they had found Jim's cap.

There were marks on the ground. It looked like something had been dragged through the bushes and toward the lake.

Lisa was never found.

Chapter 3

A Party by the Lake

A year passed.

Then a sailing club bought some land at the north end of the lake. They built a clubhouse there.

Todd loved sailing. He was one of the first people to join the club. He also loved music, dancing, and parties at the clubhouse.

One summer evening, Todd and his friends were at the sailing club. The doors and windows were open, and the music boomed over the lake. Todd walked outside to cool down. His girlfriend Simone went with him. Other people walked by the water, enjoying the cool breeze blowing off the lake.

The music stopped. Todd and Simone heard the DJ saying it was someone's birthday.

Then they heard splashing out in the middle of the lake.

"What was that?" Simone asked

"Ducks, I think. The music is keeping them awake." But Todd sounded unsure of himself.

The music started again. Todd and Simone started to go back inside.

Suddenly, they heard a scream. It was even louder than the music.

Someone was in trouble down by the lake!

Chapter 4

The Creature

Todd ran toward the screams. Other people followed him.

The screaming went on and on. They could hear a man's voice, too, yelling for help.

When Todd reached the lake, he saw three shapes in the moonlight. One was in the water, but it was too big to be human.

The shape pulled at a screaming girl. The other person was holding onto her. It was Mike, Todd's friend. Todd guessed that the girl was Rosie, Mike's girlfriend.

The creature was slowly dragging Rosie deeper into Dark Lake. Desperately, Todd looked around. He saw a pile of stones. He picked one up and threw it as hard as he could at the creature.

Other people rushed down to the lake. They saw what Todd was doing, and they started to do the same. The creature howled in rage. For a moment, Todd could see its giant head outlined against the moon.

Todd had never seen anything like it. Not in real life, anyway.

It looked like a dinosaur.

Chapter 5

Hard to Believe

The stones were too much for the creature. With a roar of anger, it let go of Rosie and then disappeared under the water. Everyone rushed to help.

Rosie was badly hurt. There were deep red marks on her legs and body. She was losing a lot of blood, but at least she was alive.

Mike called 911.

An ambulance came to take Rosie away. Mike went with her.

Then a police officer arrived and asked people what had happened. The officer didn't believe the story at first. He thought there might have been a fight, and that was how Rosie got hurt. He thought people were telling the story to cover up a fight.

Then the officer got a call on his radio. It was from the hospital.

"They think Rosie is going to be okay," the officer said. "The claw marks went very deep, though. She needs surgery."

"Claw marks!" exclaimed Todd. "Do you believe us now?"

"It's a strange story," the police officer replied. "But I don't have any other choice."

Chapter 6

DEEPS

When people heard about the creature in the lake, they remembered what had happened to Jim Small and Lisa Dahl. Could the creature have attacked them, too?

Police divers came to the lake, but they couldn't find anything.

"It's too deep for us," they said. "And the water is as thick as soup!"

A month later, a truck arrived at the clubhouse. It was towing a trailer. On the trailer was something that looked like a huge, metal fish. It was a three-person submarine called DEEP2.

The sub captain was named Jack Saunders. He talked to Todd and the others. He wanted to hear about the creature.

"We'll have the sub ready by tomorrow," he said. "Then we'll go and see what's down there. I think we'll find something interesting!"

Chapter 7

Todd Steps Forward

The next morning, everyone was at the clubhouse. A crane lowered DEEP2 into the water. Jack was ready to go on board with Carla, the copilot.

The captain looked at his watch. “Where’s Will?” he asked. “He should have been here by now.”

Will was the cameraman. He went along to take photographs and videos.

The captain's cell phone rang.

"Yes?" the captain answered his phone. "Where are you, Will? What? You're joking! Okay. Talk to you later."

"Will's sick!" the captain exclaimed. "He's got the flu! Who's going to take the pictures?"

Todd stepped forward. "I've done some photography before. I'll do it."

Chapter 8

Into the Depths

DEEP2 slipped down into the murky water. Todd was glad his parents weren't there. He was sure they would have stopped him from going.

Carla checked the depth.

"The water's about 200 feet deep."

Down they went. Jack switched on a light, but it was still hard to see anything.

At last they were close to the bottom. They could see the muddy bed of the lake.

"What's that?" Todd pointed.

He had spotted something huge and made of silver-gray metal.

It was half buried in the mud, but they could see a pair of wings at one end. There was only one thing it could be.

A spaceship!

Suddenly, there was a bang on the side of the sub. Then a crack.

They could hear the hiss of water.

One of the portholes was cracking!

Chapter 9

Let's Get Out of Here!

Outside, they could see a scaly arm with razor-sharp claws. It was holding a large rock and using it to crack the porthole. One more smash and water would come pouring in.

"Quick! Let's get out of here!" the captain ordered.

Carla tried to get the sub to go faster, but it was hard to steer. The creature was hanging onto the sub.

The creature started to move toward the front window. Its evil eyes peered in at them. They knew what it was going to do next. Smash the window! If it did that, they would have no chance of escape.

During all the excitement, Todd was taking photographs

Carla slammed the sub into reverse, and then forward, steering hard to the right.

The creature screamed, and the water turned red as the sub's propeller sliced into it.

Chapter 10

A Missing Child

Todd's pictures were all over the newspapers the next day.

"At least there won't be any more disappearing people," said the police officer.

But deep in the lake strange things were happening. In the spaceship, two mighty creatures were wondering why their youngest child hadn't come home.

THE DAILY GLOBE

ALIEN LIVES IN LAKE FOR THOUSANDS OF YEARS!

ALIEN CASTAWAY DIES IN LAKE OF EVIL

INSIDE

The huge creatures opened the hatch and set off to look for their child.

In the clubhouse, another party was under way . . .

About the Author

David Orme taught school for 18 years before becoming a full-time writer. He has written over 200 books about tornadoes, orangutans, soccer, space travel, and other topics.

In his free time, David enjoys taking his granddaughter, Sarah, on adventures to visit London graveyards. He lives in Hampshire, England, with his wife, Helen, who is also a writer.

About the Illustrator

Paul Savage works in a design studio. He says illustrating books is "the best job." He's always been interested in illustrating books, and he loves reading. Paul also enjoys playing sports and running.

He lives in England with his wife and daughter, Amelia.

Glossary

copilot (KOH-pye-luht)—the assistant pilot of an airplane or ship

crane (KRANE)—a machine with a long arm that lifts and moves heavy objects

DJ (DEE-jay)—someone who plays recorded music at a party

porthole (PORT-hohl)—a small, round window in the side of a ship or boat

propeller (pruh-PEL-ur)—a set of rotating blades that moves a vehicle through water or air

submarine (SUHB-muh-reen)—a ship that can travel both on the surface and under the water

surgery (SUR-jer-ee)—medical treatment to repair injured body parts

Discussion Questions

1. At the beginning of the story, we learn that local people believe that something evil lives in Dark Lake. Why do you think the builders ignore the warnings and build the city anyway?

2. The police officer doesn't believe Todd's story about what happened to Rosie. If you hadn't seen the creature, do you think you would believe Todd's story? Why or why not?

3. How do you think the creatures will react when they find out their child has been killed? Will they be afraid, or will they be angry? What will they do next?

Writing Prompts

1. Do you believe there are creatures living on our planet that people have never seen? Write what these creatures might look like and how they might behave.

2. Imagine you are Todd when he finds out that the cameraman is sick. Write what you would do.

3. The people living near Dark Lake think they are safe now that the creature has been killed. But the end of the story suggests there are even larger creatures still in the lake. Write a story about what you think will happen next.

Also by David Orme

Space Pirates
1-59889-016-6

The crew members of the Nightstar *are on a cargo mission in deep space when their ship is taken over. It doesn't take the crew long to discover that they are being attacked — by space pirates!*

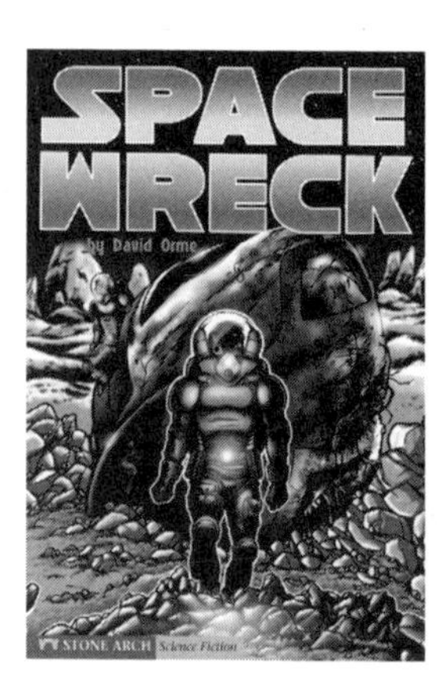

Space Wreck
1-59889-015-8

Space explorers Sam and Simon are traveling in search of space crystals when their ship suddenly loses power and crashes on an asteroid. Will Sam and Simon find a way to get off the asteroid?

Other Books in This Set

Splitzaroni
by K. I. White
1-59889-014-X

Naseem always runs for cover when his mom returns with the groceries. When she comes back with a weird new plant, it seems she might have gone too far.

Steel Eyes
by Jonny Zucker
1-59889-019-0

Emma Stone is the new girl in school. Why does she always wear sunglasses? Gail and Tanya are determined to find out, but Emma's cold stare is more than they bargained for.

Internet Sites

Do you want to know more about subjects related to this book? Or are you interested in learning about other topics? Then check out FactHound, a fun, easy way to find Internet sites.

Our investigative staff has already sniffed out great sites for you!

Here's how to use FactHound:

1. Visit *www.facthound.com*

2. Select your grade level.

3. To learn more about subjects related to this book, type in the book's ISBN number: **1598890174**.

4. Click the **Fetch It** button.

FactHound will fetch the best Internet sites for you!